CLOUDY

Deborah King

For Cloudy,
not forgetting Winnie and Mr Cat

Library of Congress Cataloging-in-Publication Data

King, Deborah, 1950–
    Cloudy.

    Summary: Follows the quiet activities of a cat
as it blends into its surroundings.
    1. Cats – Juvenile fiction. [1. Cats – Fiction]
I. Title
PZ10.3.K559CL 1989 [E]   89-8704
ISBN 0-399-22242-1

CLOUDY
Deborah King

PHILOMEL BOOKS

New York

I am a little gray cat called Cloudy.
I am the color of thunder and rain.
It's difficult to see me on dull days.

When the rain pours, you may catch sight of me in murky puddles.

When the wind blows, I am swept away like
a ball of fluff.

If the sun shines, I stalk in the shadows.

Before, when I was wild, I slept in a stable.

I lurked in tumbledown sheds and dark alleys.

I rolled in the dirt and would disappear in a cloud of dust.

Now, I sit by a warm stove on a winter's evening,
but still no one knows I am there.

On summer mornings, I hide in the top of the
plum tree where the birds can't see me.

I hunt at dusk.

I prowl through the long grass under the light of the moon.

I run like the wind.

When I come home, I creep through my
front door, silently, secretly.
No one notices.

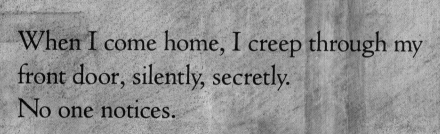

No one, that is, except my old friend, who keeps my secret until the first misty light of dawn…

...when I disappear again.